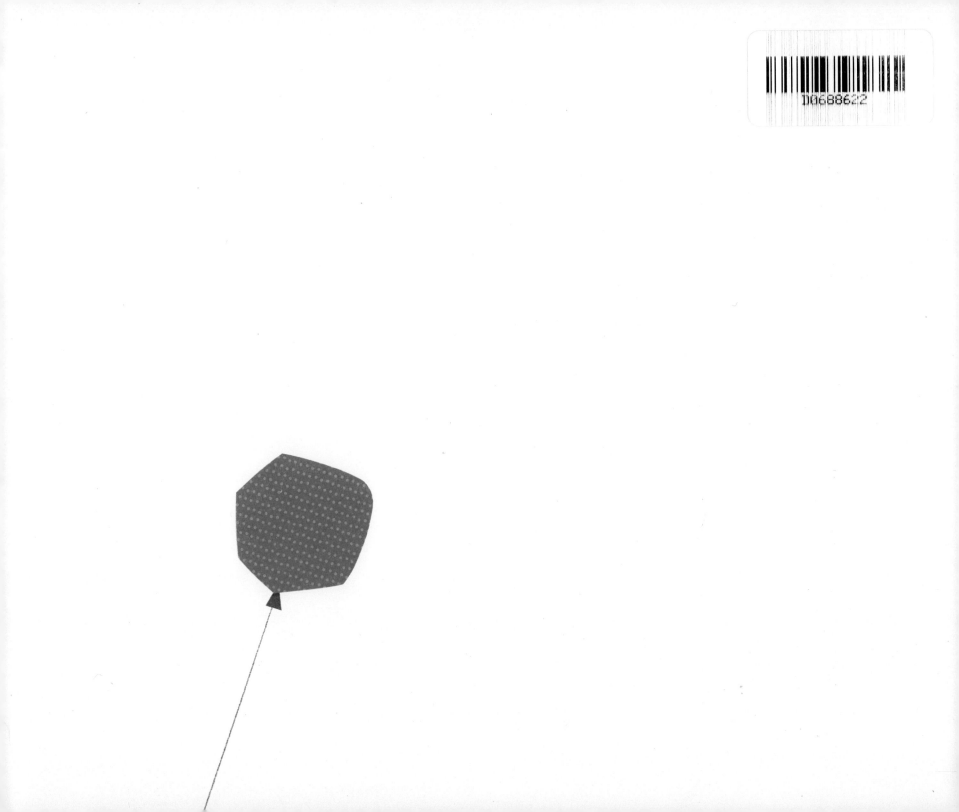

SKUNK ON A STRING

written and illustrated by
THAO LAM

Owlkids Books

To Jon—thank you for showing me what is possible through teamwork and love.
And Maddie—can't believe something so cute can be so stinky.

Story and illustrations © 2016 Thao Lam

Owlkids Books acknowledges the financial support of the Canada Council for the Arts, the Ontario Arts Council, the Government of Canada through the Canada Book Fund (CBF) and the Government of Ontario through the Ontario Media Development Corporation's Book Initiative for our publishing activities.

Published in Canada by
Owlkids Books Inc.
10 Lower Spadina Avenue
Toronto, ON M5V 2Z2

Published in the United States by
Owlkids Books Inc.
1700 Fourth Street
Berkeley, CA 94710

Library and Archives Canada Cataloguing in Publication

Lam, Thao, author, illustrator
    Skunk on a string / written and illustrated by Thao Lam.

ISBN 978-1-77147-131-2 (bound)

    I. Title.

PS8623.A466S58 2016   jC813'.6   C2015-905534-2

Library of Congress Control Number: 2015948452

Edited by: Jessica Burgess
Designed by: Alisa Baldwin

ONTARIO ARTS COUNCIL
CONSEIL DES ARTS DE L'ONTARIO
an Ontario government agency
un organisme du gouvernement de l'Ontario

Canada Council
for the Arts

Conseil des Arts
du Canada

Canadä

Manufactured in Shenzhen, Guangdong, China, in October 2015, by WKT Co. Ltd.
Job #15CB1045

A   B   C   D   E   F

 Publisher of Chirp, chickaDEE and OWL
www.owlkidsbooks.com | Owlkids Books is a division of   Bayard
CANADA

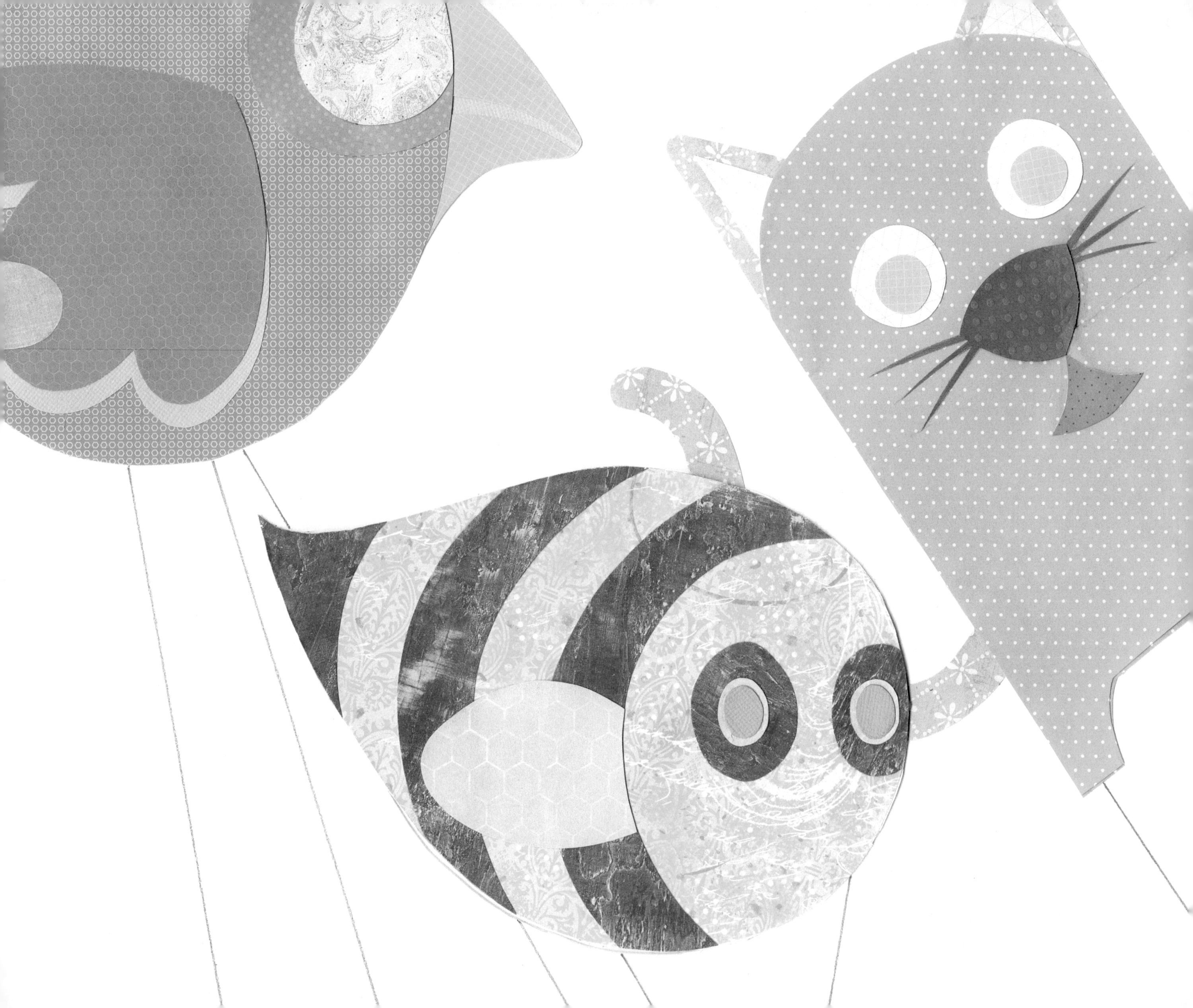

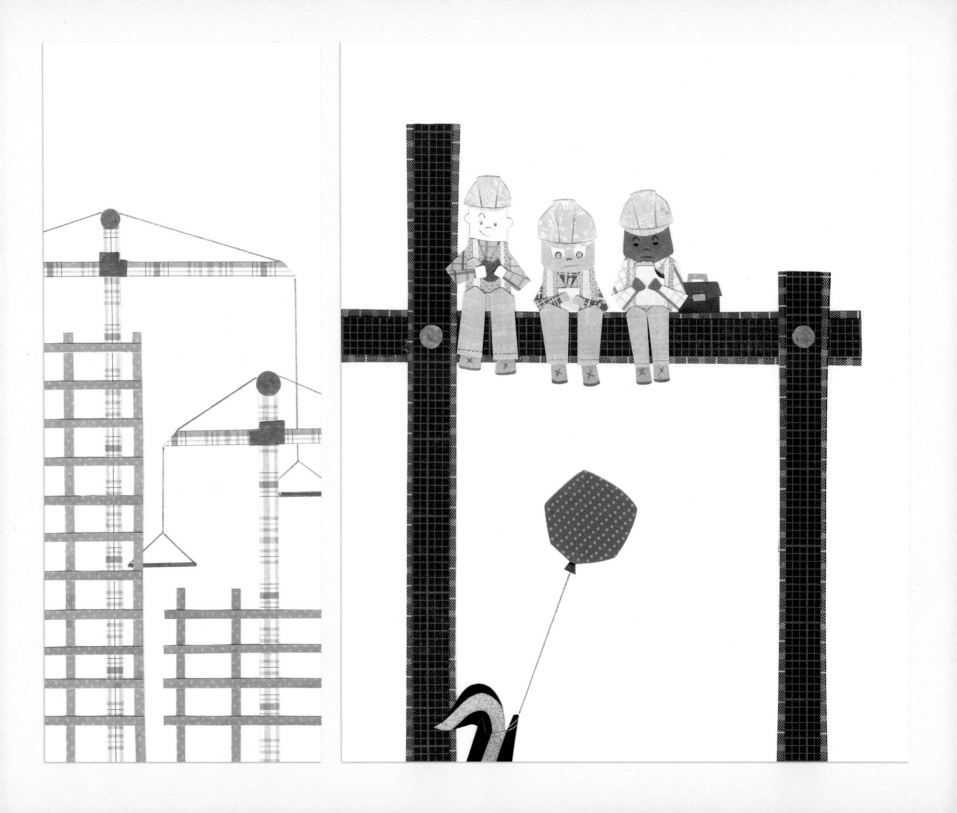

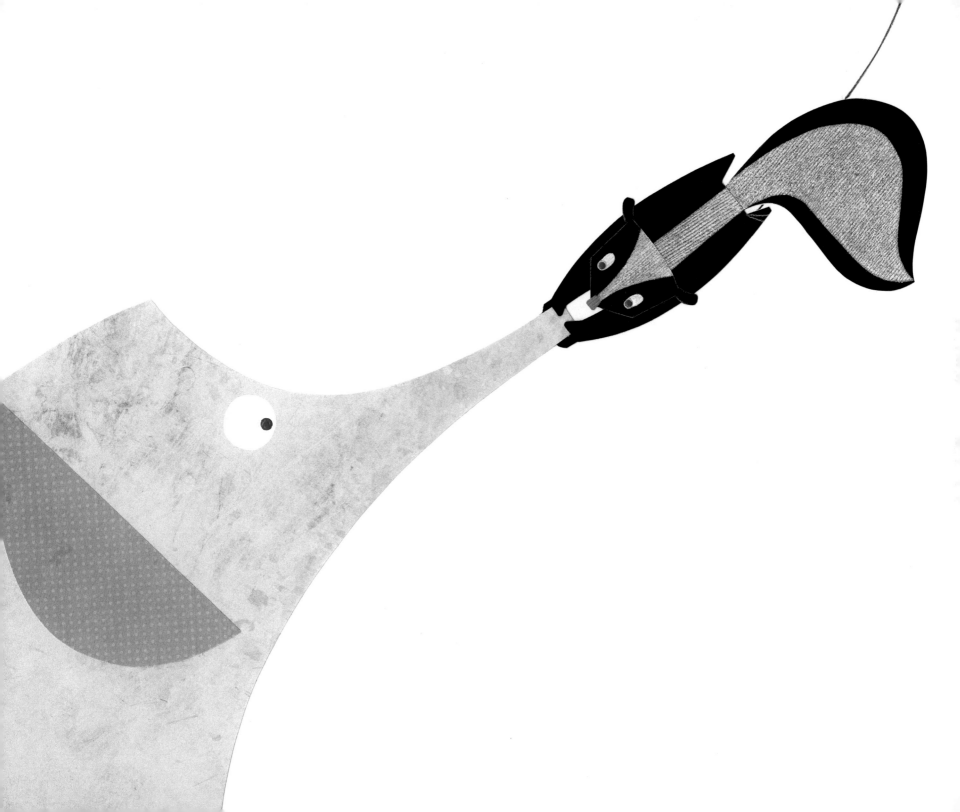

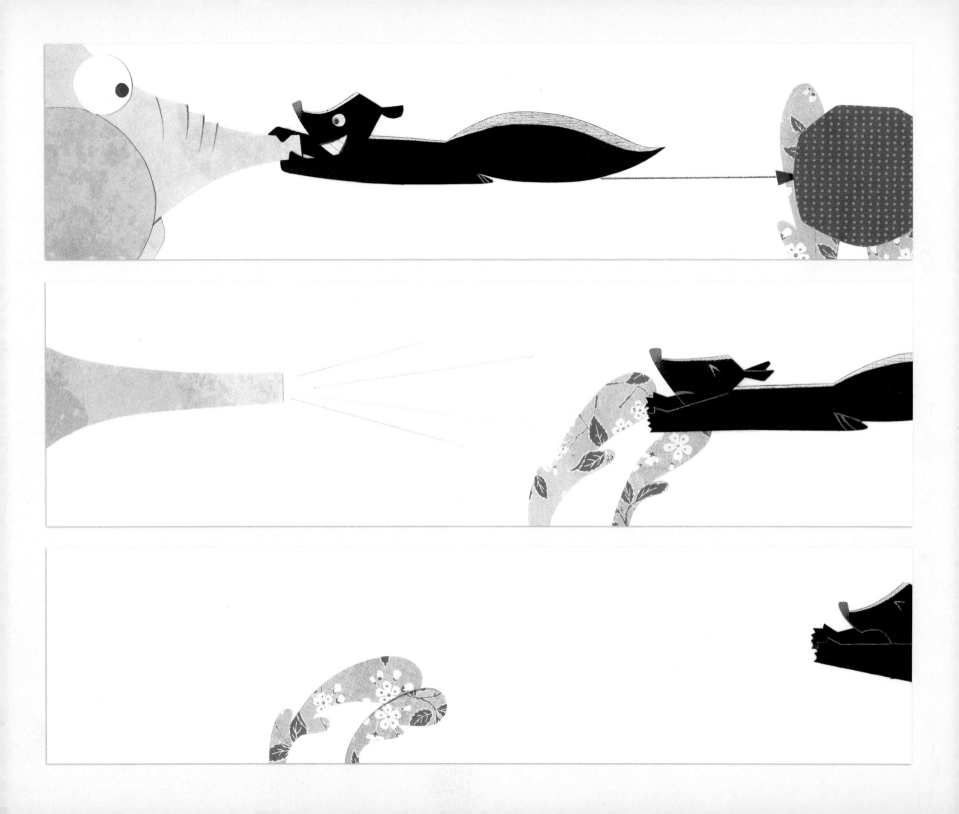

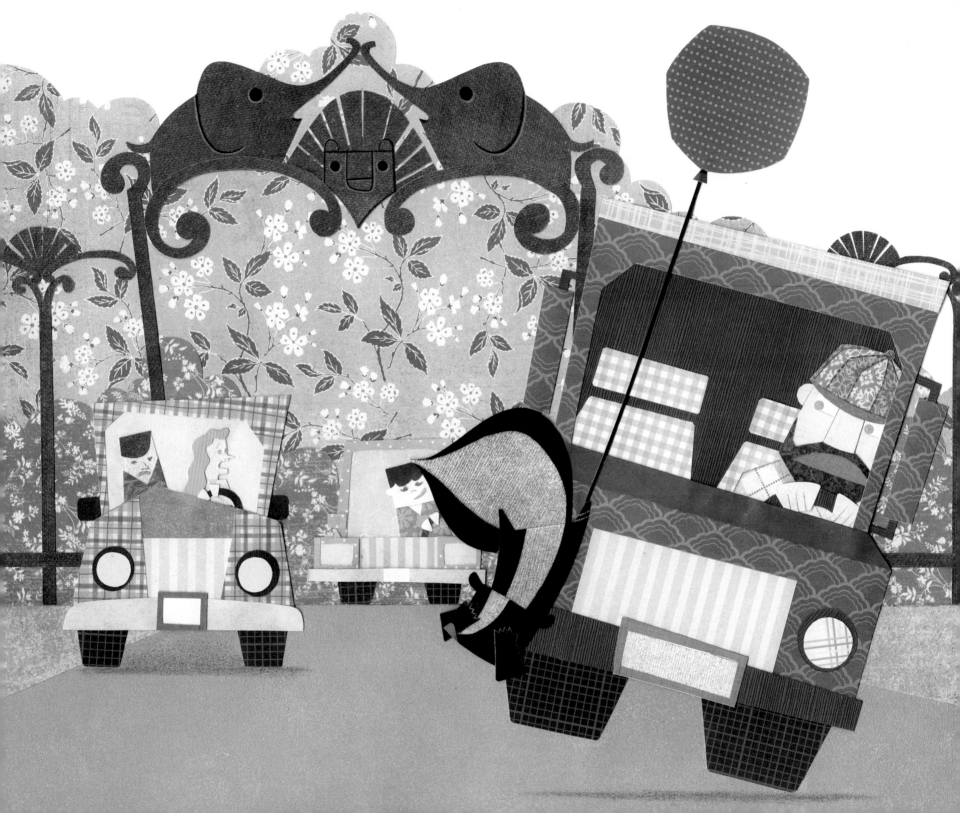

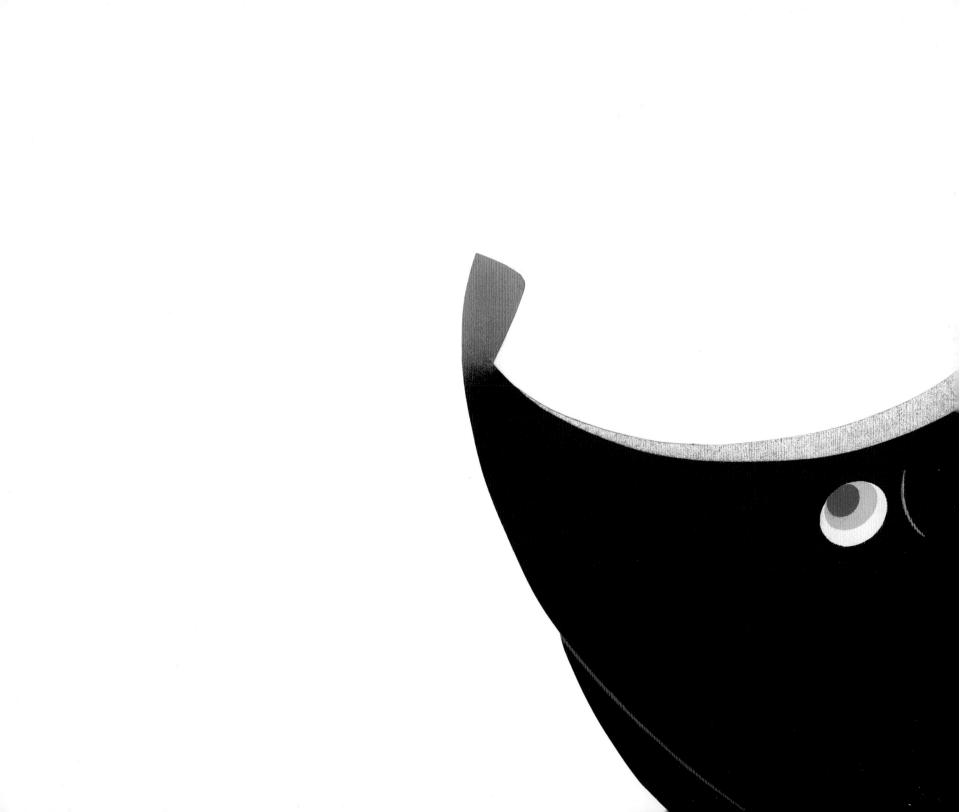